6/29/88
To Corey
with love—
Big Jim & Nancy

Apricot ABC

An Atlantic Monthly Press Book

Little, Brown and Company   Boston   Toronto

Weekly Reader Children's Book Club presents

Apricot ABC

by
Miska Miles

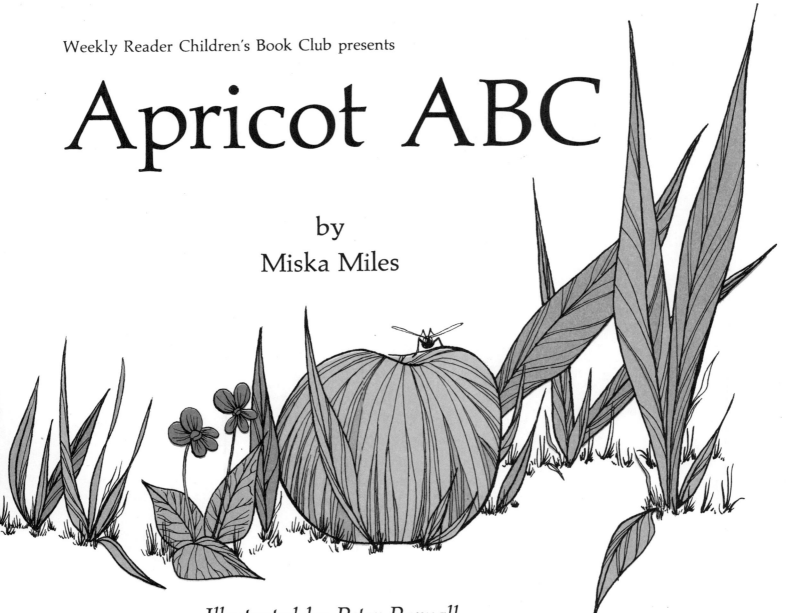

Illustrated by Peter Parnall

Books by Miska Miles

KICKAPOO

DUSTY AND THE FIDDLERS

SEE A WHITE HORSE

PONY IN THE SCHOOLHOUSE

MISSISSIPPI POSSUM

FOX AND THE FIRE

TEACHER'S PET

RABBIT GARDEN

THE PIECES OF HOME

UNCLE FONZO'S FORD

NOBODY'S CAT

THE APRICOT A B C

LIBRARY OF CONGRESS CATALOG CARD NO. 68–22072

TR 05008 37 H2
LB 04747 23 FI

ATLANTIC–LITTLE, BROWN BOOKS
ARE PUBLISHED BY
LITTLE, BROWN AND COMPANY
IN ASSOCIATION WITH
THE ATLANTIC MONTHLY PRESS

Published simultaneously in Canada
by Little, Brown & Company (Canada) Limited

PRINTED IN THE UNITED STATES OF AMERICA

WEEKLY READER CHILDREN'S BOOK CLUB EDITION

To Owen Leavitt Thomas

An apricot tree grew knobby and tall

Beside a rickety garden wall.

A yellow-ripe apricot fell from that tree.

Swift as an arrow,

Just missing a sparrow,

It startled a

Hummingbird darted away toward the heather
Where crickets and earwigs huddled together.

Inchworm measured his way to shelter,
And insects scurried off helter-skelter,
For secret places in ivy and brush—

Quiet—quiet—hush—hush—

Bee. The bee buzzed busily, "Come and see
The beautiful fruit of the apricot tree."

Crickets and butterflies came to look.

Caterpillars, all hump and crook,

Crawled from the

Dillweed down by the brook.

Dragonfly flew to a twig nearby.

A beetle came, and a damselfly.

Earthworm wriggled out of the ground,
Eager to find what the bee had found.

Feathers fluffed, a hen came along,
Contentedly clucking a favorite song,
Little and sweet.

"Look at her feet!" said a fat little frog.
"She's a monster! Hurry! Hide under a log!"

Grasshoppers crouched on a gooseberry stem.
"Hide in the grass," frog said to them.

Junebug crawled in a jasmine thicket,

And a juniper sheltered a worried cricket.

Katydids and big-eyed flies
Watched that hen of enormous size.
The hen kicked out with her bright yellow feet,
Hunting kernels of corn and grains of wheat.

Under a leaf lay the apricot.

Hen tasted the fruit and liked it a lot.
"A lovely lunch. A delicious bit."
She clucked with pleasure as she pecked at it.

"A magnificent meal. A marvel, indeed."
And she ate right down to the apricot seed.

She fluttered her wings and shook her breast
And stalked back home to sit on her nest
Where she laid a new egg and then settled to rest.

Out from their hiding, into the sun
All little creatures came one by one.

Through oleander and wild blue myrtle
Came hornet and cricket and a lazy old turtle.
A fly walked about on a

Peanut plant.

While up its stem crawled a shiny ant.

Quietly, from special places

In the flickering shadow of Queen Anne's laces,
Quickly ventured queer little things,
On fluttering, fragile gossamer wings.

Rabbit stopped for a minute or two
And nibbled at the meadow rue,
While near the old tree in a pleasant spot
Lay the rough little,
cool little,
apricot

Seed. Sowbugs rolled up tight and small

And a sparrow sang from the garden wall.

Turtle and titmouse found places to sleep

There among creatures that crawl and creep.

Up stems of dillweed, down stalks of dock,

Under the ivy, over a rock,

Busy they were, this warm summer's day,

Now that the hen had gone away.

Along a vine or under a log,
Through the meadow, or down by the bog,

They crept through the purple violet bed
Where a spider hung a silver thread
And fastened it to a Jimsonweed,
And spun a

Web above that seed

Where it lies near its tree in a sheltered spot,

That brown-pink seed of the apricot.

The spider's web makes a shimmering X
Above the seed. Exquisite flecks
Of violet blooms are drifting down,
And the Jimsonweed is dry and brown.

Yellow sun shines. Wind huffs and heaves
And covers the seed with yellowed leaves
And a dollop of dirt and a smidgin of sand.
Then frost lies lightly on the land.

Rains zig and zag and breezes blow,
Helping that little seed to grow.
And up from the ground, one day there will be
In that very same place,

A YOUNG APRICOT TREE.

Young tree will flower, fruit will grow,
While crickets click and roosters crow
And sparrows cheep
And locusts leap.
Young fruit will ripen in the sun
And busy creatures, one by one,
Will hop or jump or creep to see
Yellow-ripe apricots fall from the tree.